Trained Thoughts Publishing Presents

I0537717

Sex Assassin

Almondo Scott

Table of Contents

Prologue

It's now 1:36 am and Sharday: The Sex Assassin was victorious again because she drained Diego dick bone dry and it's limp as hell with no chance of return she watched him sit there then she cleaned up, locked up and left him and his limp dick .On her way to her car she checked her phone, but was surprised no calls from Zack at all. So, she texted him you woke. Zack hears his phone but was super busy, so he couldn't answer.

Zella busted three nuts while riding Zack face and right after the 3rd one he grabbed her ass cheeks and was bouncing her on his tongue as she moaned "Yes daddy eat it, eat it, fuuuuck, I'm Cumming, as she laid her hands on his chest while stroking his tongue, she moans.

"I want that dick." Zella says.

"Take it then." Zack says while smiling then gets up licks all her juices off his lips and jumps on his dick slowly because it's too much to force it all at once.

After Zack didn't reply Sharday returned Flex message.

"What's happening." Sharday says.

"Stranger danger what's good.' Flex says.

"Shit chilling wyd."

"Just woke up on some hungry shit."

"Oh yea, you going to cook something."

"Hell, naw about to make me a sandwich and go back to sleep, unless you going to stop by."

" Idk, you might be trying to take my goodies." Sharday says as she laughs.

"It's not taking if you give it to me."

"Whatever I'll be there in 15 min."

"Bet call me when u close, I should be woke."

So, Sharday cleans up and heads out of Diego house, as he snores, and she laughs.

Sharday opens up the video message from O Damn, and she was shocked as hell.

Chapter 1: How it all Started

Sharday opens her eyes and looks at the mirrors on the ceiling and says to herself.

" Wheeew that boy Flex is now in my top because he did stuff to my body that I didn't think was humanly possible, plus he didn't talk shit like I was and just because I made him tap out 2x the first time we fucked but I must say he held his ground and I knew he had potential to be a great fuck… but damn not that good of a fuck." Sharday says to herself while laying in the bed.

Oh, by the way I'm Sharday and welcome to the Sex Assassin.

So as Sharday sits up in the bed, looking around and says to herself. I'm going to need this bed for twenty more minutes, rolls over to layback down, opens her eyes and notice her bra was hanging on the lamp, her dress was on the balcony door handle, one heel in the chair and the other one was hanging on the night stand knob by the string that ties around the ankle…before it finally fell and hit the floor.

"Wait a minute where are my panties." As she raises the covers to see them twisted around her big toe. She dropped her head back down on the pillow.

"No more Tequila for me." Sharday says as her phone rings and she jumps up.

"Damn that alarm is load as hell wtf". As she knocks the phone on the floor then it shuts off. But then the phone ringed again it was a phone call, she answers it.

"Hello." Sharday says with the drunk voice.

"Hey superwoman how are you this am." Flex says.

"Shut up fool and why are you so loud Jesus Christ." Sharday says.

"That's the same thing I was asking you last night, lol." Flex says while laughing.

"Shut up fool."

"Get yo ass up and hit me back punk." Flex says after giggles.

"Aight bet." Sharday says as she finally sits up in bed.

As Sharday pieces together all of her clothes, washes her face, brushed her teeth, and heads out the house as her eyes was murdered by the sun as she makes it to her car. So, she goes home so she can take a bath and continue the rest of her day, but before she showers, she checks her phone to see five messages, eight missed calls and two voicemails, she smiles and checks the voicemails first.

First voicemail was from someone she labeled #1 because he was the first guy to have her do everything for the first time and his name was O'Dell, but she nicknamed him O'Damn because at times he has left her saying those exact words.

Second voicemail was from someone she would do anything at the drop of a hat because he had as special place in her heart because of the things he did for her just after knowing her for two months after they met, and his name is Zack "the Pleaser."

So, O'Dell was three of the missed calls and three of the messages.

Zack was two of the missed calls and two of the messages.

The other three missed calls were private numbers.

Sharday looks at the messages after checking her voicemail and all she could say was, "you got to be shitting me, lol".

The three private calls was from this guy she met at the lounge last weekend, they switched numbers, hung out a couple times, fukked once and she made him tap out super early because she put a move she been practicing on him and it worked, lol. So at this point he trying to redeem himself, so she figured she would call him back because he was two of the messages and he made it very clear that he was trying to see her asap so he could prove what happened the first time was a fluke. But she just don't he ready because he is the guy with the strong shit talking game, but his dick game is not equal to his shit talking. So, she decides to reply anyway.

She never told the shit talker his dick game was wack she just curved him, and she vowed to herself if he ever called her more than three times in one day she would let him know why he has no right to be calling her so much, then she spoke him up because he called.

"What's happening." Sharday says while smiling.

"Hey stranger, what's going on." Shit talker says while laughing.

"What up, who is this." Sharday says as she looks at the phone to see the number.

"Diego."

"Diego from." Sharday says.

"Boom Boom Room on 33rd street". Diego says.

"Aww hey." She says with the ugh face.

"You don't sound too excited to hear from me."

"Well actually you never done nothing to me to make me excited about hearing from you." Sharday says while laughing.

"Lmao, wow well what you doing later on."

"Idk maybe going to get my brains fukked out by my sexual hero". Sharday says as she laughs.

"Quit playing, for real wyd though."

"LMAO, What the hell you laughing at I'm deadass". Sharday as she laughs at him.

"Aw damn ok, so when can I see you." Diego ask.

Then her other line clicks.

"Hold on for a second." Sharday says.

"OK."

It was Zack asking her to see her and she says ok.

"Diego let me hit you back in a minute."

"Ok well at least think about what I asked."

"Ok gotcha". Sharday says as she gets her change of clothes together before she gets ready to shower, and then her phone rings, it was O'Dell.

"Hey miss kitty."

"Hey O'Dell, how are you doing today."

"I'm cool so when can I see you."

"When you want to see me." Sharday says as she smiles.

"Tonight, I got something for you."

"Ok I'm going to call you when I'm on my way later on." Sharday says while giggling.

"Ok cool, that will work"

She goes to run the shower and comes back to a message from Flex, you know the same guy from that wild night she had in the beginning. And he was telling her how that pussy was on point and how he loved how she disrespected that dick, that shit left him speechless not to mention that kitty stayed juicy the whole time he was eating that ass from the back while fingering that pussy.

She smiled shivered and caught chills just thinking about that night.

"Actually, Zack might have to wait till after I go see Flex because he talking some shit, and I want see what he want to give me lol." Sharday says while smiling.

So, she finally has the chance to shower and use her new shower head, lol.

As soon as she got out the shower and was sitting on the bed putting lotion on, Flex texted her, and after soon after Zack calls her.

"Hello." Sharday says.

"I miss you let's get lunch." Zack asks Sharday.

"Oh, damn that was a different way to reply, lol. Ok I can do that, what time you talking about." Sharday asks him.

"Ijs, I'm working around your availability, so let me know what time is good for you." Zack says.

"Ok that's cool, I will be in touch." Sharday says.

"Fosho." Zack replies.

She says ok because that will get him out the way early so, she can go see Flex later that evening, lol. She puts her phone on the charger and lays down to figure out this masterplan but at the same time Diego thirsty ass keep texting her, she laughs and rolls over.

"So, who can I call over to put me to sleep." Sharday says as she smiles, then she feels her pussy throbbing like a heartbeat just thinking about some dick penetrating her Juicebox.

"Let me see, O'Dell, Zack or Diego, decisions, decisions, you know what I will sleep on it." She says as she rolls over and takes a nap. Because she has to figure out who would be the most fun out of each one of them, with the fact she has history with them all.

Chapter 2: Let the fun begin

So Sharday woke up from a freaky ass dream that left the back of her legs and her forehead dripping with sweat, not to mention her pussy had accumulated some extra juices while she was sleeping and dreaming. Plus, her doorbells were poking through one side of her tank top while the other titty had slide out of the whole tank top. She laughed, then her phone vibrated, and she had 4 picture messages and three videos.

Flex sent her two picture messages of him in the shower and one video message of that night they had because when he was telling her how much noise she was making, and how she was running from the dick at first. she didn't believe him, so he had to prove it to her. She was so embarrassed, and she messaged him that and he told her not to be its cool.

"Wow you petty as hell, Omg I'm so embarrassed." Sharday says.

"Lmao, you good don't be, just next time bring your training shoes, your face in the pillow too lol." Flex says while laughing.

"Fuck you asshole." Sharday replies as she tries to wake up all the way.

Then she looked at the two videos and one picture message that O'Dell sent her.

The first video was her riding him till he busted so many nuts he went to sleep right after. And the other video was the threesome they had with her friend and the picture was his dick covered with all that cream she covered his dick with. Then she messaged him back.

"Omg that night with her was fukking awesomely amazing and we need to get hold of her again, she was a lot of fun". Sharday say as she smiles hard as hell.

He sent back smiley emojis

"That's the night I made you tap out." Odell says while giggling.

"Ok you up one, but not for long." Sharday says.

"You ready for rounds three, four and five, lol." O'Dell says.

"Hell, yea but this time I'm going to be the winner I got something for yo ass." She says as she putting her clothes on.

Then there was two more pics, and they were from Diego, she didn't even open up those messages.

"Damn OMG his thirsty, lol." She says while smiling.

But while putting on her perfume she went back to the video O'Dell sent her, "mmm, mmm, mmm whew." Sharday says as she grins and looks at Flex picture message again and turns the phone sideways.

"My, My, My I must say that man is blessed."

Ok so I know you have noticed that Sharday has an extremely high sex drive/border line nympho. And she has yet came across a someone that can sexually punish her, without her coming back for a rematch the same night and forcing a round three and four that will make her record for the night 3-1, her way. But she is in for a rude awakening this time.

So, Sharday Finally leaves the house because she had a couple things to take care of this afternoon, then she decides to call Flex as soon as she got in her car, because of those pics he sent her.

"What up stranger." Sharday text Flex as she smiles.

"Hey, screaming moaner, how are you today." Flex says.

"I'm Good and lol you got jokes huh, well I got something for your ass, mister baby please stop I'm not ready to explode." Sharday says while laughing as flex face drops after she tried to throw shade.

"And you was saying... don't get silent now" Sharday says as she giggles.

"I got yo ass, lol." Flex says while laughing.

"I mean I must say, you got skills, but the difference is I'm talented, and talent beats skills any day."

"OOH you talking big shit too, ok cool and we will see."

"Now you know you can't talk shit to a shit talker, lil buddy you better recognize the power of the P.U.S.S.Y."

"All I have to say is when can I see you."

"IDK you sure you ready."

"I'm Positive motherfukker."

"OK give me a second let me check my availability, I will keep you posted." Sharday says.

"Do that because I'm on good bullshit with yo ass." Flex says while laughing.

"Boy I'm not worried about yo ass, lol I'm about to check and I will ttyl." Sharday says.

"Fosho."

Sharday is on her way to her destination and receives a message from Zack.

"Still waiting." Zack says.

Then she calls Zack back.

"My bad I was taking care of something." Sharday says.

"It's cool, how is your day so far young lady." Zack asks.

"It's cool handsome how is your day so far."

"It's actually going great so far, I can't complain wyd now."

"Nothing now chilling in the car under this air, because this ninety-degrees feels lie a hundred."

"You want to meet me at Plattos for lunch in about an hour or whatever time is good for."

"That's cool 3:30-4 is cool."

"Ok well I will see you in a little while."

"Ok see you soon."

As soon as she hung up the phone, she noticed the chill bumps that appeared on her arm, as she smiled thinking about seeing him later on.

"This man does something to me, OMG and to think I almost had real feelings for him, but I had to gather myself. But I must say he is a decent fuck, but his personality make him the best." Sharday says to herself before she snaps out of it.

"Girl calm yo ass down woosah and go get that free meal, lol." She says to herself. As she got herself together

So, O'Dell was in the mall and sees Zella the one him and Sharday had a threesome with a while back, so he creeps up behind her.

"Damn that ass phat." O'Dell said as he sees her from the back.

She turns around laughing because she knew who it was just by the sound of his voice.

"Hey handsome." Zella smiles as she greets O'Dell with a big hug.

"What's up stranger how you been."

"Chilling and working what you been up too." Zella says as she smiles and puts her hands on her hips.

"You know what's crazy, me and Sharday was just talking about you."

Zella gives him the side eye

"Lol Oh, really, and I wonder what yall was talking about." Zella says as she puts her hands on her hips.

"You already know, the good times we use to have, how we kicked it that night and how we need to get hold of you real soon." O'Dell says while grinning.

"Mmmm, hmm sounds like someone miss me." Zella says while cheesing ear to ear.

"Whatever punk, you talked to Sharday." O'Dell asks her.

"It's been a minute like a week or two, I just been really busy, but I been meaning to call her." Zella says.

"Well make that happen, call her and let's make some more magical moments." O'Dell says as Zella looks at him and bites her finger and smiles.

"Aight take my number down."

"Ok I got it, that's me calling you now, I'm going to hit you later to see if you want to hang out with us, because I suppose to see her later."

"Aight bet."

"Yea set that up so we can make more magical moments."

"Ok cool I'm with it, and if I did have plans, I would cancel to kick it with the two of yall, LOL." Zella says as she gives him a hug and he grabs two hand full of her ass.

"Don't you start nothing you can't finish." Zella says while giving him the seductive look in her eyes as they smiled at each other as they went their separate ways. As Zella looked at him seductively as she walked away, while shaking that ass, and he noticed it and smiled.

Then O'Dell text Sharday.

"You want to take down Zella tonight."

"Hell, yea set that shit up."

So Sharday finally makes to her destination, sits in her car going through her phone checking messages and replies to O'Dell message, and calls Zella.

"Hey boo wyd." Zella says.

"Hey lovely, shit in this car looking for my shirt I bought last week, what you been up to stranger." Sharday ask.

"Shit working that's about it, girls guess who I ran into in the mall earlier today."

"Somebody we went to school with, um David with the mole on his nose." Sharday asks while laughing.

"Girl hell no, O'Dell." Zella says in excitement.

"Wow that's funny as hell because we was just talking about you the other day, and what he do this time." Sharday asks while laughing.

"Funny Because he told me that and nothing until I gave him my number and said goodbye, then he grabbed two hand full of my ass when he gave me a hug and baby the way he grabbed this ass I had an instant flashback of that night we had last time we linked up, and my shit got me wet." Zella says after saying whew.

"Ikr, He something else."

"He was telling me ya'll was supposed to get together today."

"Now You know you are more than welcome to join us, so stop being a stranger and come fuck with us." Sharday says as she giggles.

"Oh, hell yea I'm going to do that and if I did have plans, I would have cancelled to kick it with two of yall." Zella says while laughing.

"Ok well let's make it happen boo, I can't wait to see you lol."

"Same here, well just hit me up with location."

"Better believe I'm going to do that."

So, after Sharday finished talking to Zella she sees a text from Zack with the location and address to where they can meet up at, she headed there and while she was parking she saw Zack pulling up across the street about to park, then she screams out at him.

"Hey cutie can I get your number." Sharday yells out as Zack sees her and starts smiling as she makes her way across the street to Plattos. She greets him with a hug as he kisses her on her cheek and speaks to her in a soft tone.

"Damn you looking good and smelling good today." Zack says while smiling and looking her up and down admiring her beauty.

Sharday smiles ear to ear as he does what he normally does and lets her walk-in front of him as he holds the door open for her as they enter the restaurant. And he continues chivalry like he was raised and once they made it to their seats before she could raise her hands, he pulled out her seat for her, she smiles as he continued by letting her order first as she smiles harder than the first time. At that moment she realized what made her fall in love with him in the first place he is a complete gentleman. So, they get situated and order their food and talk because Zack does not allow cell phones on dates, because it takes away from real life conversation. So, she knew to leave her phone in the car. But while her phone was in the car, she received messages from O'Dell and then the conversation with Zack begin.

Then Flex texted her and asked if he could have her for dinner, as the waiter brings them some water.

"I will be right back to take you all order." Waiter says.

"Ok, So Sharday tell me something good." Zack asks Sharday.

"I missed you." Sharday says as she smiles.

"Oh, is that so." Zack says as he smiles in shock.

"Yes." Sharday says.

"Where did that come from, and where did those feelings come from." Zack ask Sharday.

"Honestly, I like you, but I love the way you treat me is just awesome and sometimes I be wondering." Sharday says as she sips her water.

"What was you wondering though." Zack asks her as he drops lemons in his water and looking at her smiling.

Sharday smiles as she looks at him.

"Sometimes I be wondering what my life would have been like if you never showed me what it was like to be loved and cared about." Sharday says.

"So, wait you never been loved, had no one to really show you that they care about you or treat you how a woman supposed to be treated." Zack says as he folds his arms and sit back to wait for her response.

"Yes, I have, but treated like a queen and no." Sharday says as her facial expression changed dramatically.

Zack smiles and grins

"Now you know I rock with you hard as hell since the day I met you and I knew how you should and how I wanted to treat you, so I made it my business to do exactly that." Zack says as Sharday smiles as she puts her hands on her face and smiles.

Then Flex text her again, as she begin asking Zack questions and Zella calls O'Dell. But we know the real reason Sharday didn't reply.

"What's happening freak body." O'Dell says.

"Shit what you on buddy." Zella responds.

"Shit about to wash my car, why you want to help me."

"IDK Depends on how much you paying." Zella says while giggling.

"Well that depends on what you are wearing while you washing it."

"Now that depends on how much you are paying lol."

"Ok well bring yo ass and when you get here, we can talk business." O'Dell says while laughing.

"Ok I will be there in 30 minutes."

"Fosho You Still have my location."

"Yea I will never forgot how to get to the fun place lol." Zella says while laughing.

"Ok I'm here."

"OK, cool I'm omw."

Diego calls Sharday two times and sent her a text message, but still no reply. And the conversation between Zack and Sharday got heated really quick.

"Can I ask you a question. Sharday asked Zack.

"Sure, Go for it." Zack replies as he sips his water.

As the waiter brings water, bread, and butter.

"Ready to order yet." Waiter Says.

"Yes, I will have the porterhouse lamb, with broccoli and Spanish rice."

"Ok, and for you sir." Waiter asks Zack.

"I will have the lemon crushed catfish, with asparagus and white cheddar potatoes." Zack says as he hands the menu to the waiter.

"Ok thank you and that will be right up." Waiter says.

"Ok, as long as we been messing around have you ever thought about what you like or hate about me, I mean even what is it we are doing." Sharday ask him.

"Yes and no." Zack says while smiling.

Sharday folds her arms and smiles

"And the yes is for." Sharday says as she butters her bread.

"Yes, because I have thought about it since we been kicking it, and we both been in and out of relationships. And as far as what I like and hate about you actually that's not the nature of our relationship because I don't have the right to judge so I just play my part." Zack explains as he grabs some bread and Sharday passes him the butter.

Then she looks at him while talking to herself (this nigga a motherfukker, godddamn, and to make it even worst he knows his role.)

"Why you looking like that." Zack ask her.

"No reason just shocked at your response that's all." Sharday says while smiling.

"I mean you know me well, so I'm not going to sugar coat shit plus, when I told you I was getting engaged you didn't judge me, you still wished me the best and at the same time told me "just because you getting married doesn't mean you're going anywhere.

Sharday smiles and laughs.

"Damn straight because that dick was mines before she came and it's going to be mines when she leaves." Sharday says as she smiles.

Zack laughs

"Wow like really that's how you feel." Zack says while smiling.

"Hell, yea and do it look like I'm laughing." Sharday says as she places her hands on the table aggressively and smirks.

"Naw, I can tell you deadass by the way you put your hands down on the table, lol." Zack as he laughs.

So their food finally came and they ate and talked a little more after eating and even manage to get in some PDA at the table in such a way it bothered the both of them so bad Sharday started getting wet from the kisses and rubbing on his dick.

So, she gets up from the table and grabs his hand and pulls him up and goes to the side by the exit. And starts to kiss him more.

"Oooh I can see you feeling some kind of way by how you kissing me." Zack says as he stands back and looks at her while she still has her hand on his shirt as she pulls him closer and kissed him more.

"But the question is what are you going to do about it." Sharday says as Zack looks shocked and surprised.

"Waiter can we have some to go boxes and the bill please." Sharday says.

"Ok I will be right back". Waiter says as she smiles.

"Wait we leaving already." Zack asks Sharday.

"Hell yea, because you about to give me some of that dick". Sharday says with aggression.

"Ok let's make it happen." Zack smiles and laughs as the waiter brings the to go boxes and the bill.

"I know you are so meet my at the car." Sharday says and smiles as she gets up and heads toward the exit.

Minutes later, after Zack paid the bill and grabbed their food, as he headed to her car. Soon as she opened the door her phone was going off, she had 3 messages and 2 missed calls, but before she sat the phone down she received another call, she sent it to voicemail and jumped in the back seat right before Zack got into the car. Soon as he closed the door she pushed both seats up and jumped on him and starting kissing him as she was unbuckling his pants, and started devouring his dick as he closed his eyes and leaned his head back, while grabbing her head saying shiiit, fuuuck, but after twenty minutes he wanted to taste that pussy, So when she finally took a break he grabbed her arms and pushed her to the other side of the back seat, pulled up her dress and started eating that thang while fingering her as she sucks her titties with one hand and controlling his head with the other hand while moaning "oooh daddy eat that pussy, then I want to paint that dick daddy" as he stopped sucking her clit and came up as she sucked the finger he was fingering her with then she tongue kissed him and jumped on his dick and rode him until she covered his dick with her cream from bussing three nuts then she licked and cleaned all her cream off his dick as she continued to suck until he came and she caught every drop.

"Wheeew I needed that." Sharday says while smiling as she grabs her wipes from under her seat.

"That makes two of us." Zack says while giggling as he buckles his pants up as they went back into the restaurant to get a drink.

They sat their smiling waiting on their drinks as Zack starts so suck on the finger that he was fingering her with as She starts smiling. So, they finished their drinks and left out got in their cars and went their separate ways. Soon as she got back in her car her voicemail was going off, again.

The three messages was from Diego, Flex and O'Damn. And the calls was from Flex and Diego and the voicemail was from Flex. So once she got situated in her car, she texted O'Damn back and said hell yea, responded to Diego like really dude and then called Flex back and they talked nasty and freaky shit on the phone for about twenty minutes, and the conversation got so heated she stopped him in mid-sentence:

"Ok enough of all this talk, when can I flood your face." Sharday says so serious.

"Let's do it asap." Flex says while laughing.

"Ok don't threaten me with a good time, in route right now heading your way." Sharday says as she heads over Flex house.

"Fosho you know where I'm at." Flex says as he hangs up the phone.

Diego text her back

"Is that a yes." Diego asks.

"No, it is what I said like really dude, nowhere near a yes dude." Sharday says with anger.

"Damn why you sound so mad."

Sharday looks at her phone laughs but doesn't reply to him but replied to O'Damn response.

"Oh, hell yea I want to, plus I owe Zella sexy ass, lol and as far as you are concerned, I want part of everything that has to do with you sexually, lol." Sharday says while smiling.

"Ok about to set it up." O'Damn says as Sharday gives him the thumbs up emoji.

So, Zella was on her was on her way to O'Dell house and she had on her carwash outfit and I must say it was fire. So, as she pulled up in his driveway, she seen him getting the bucket, soap, and water hose out then she screams out.

"Can I get a wash next." Zella says as he looks up smiles and giggles.

"Yea in the shower." O'Dell says while laughing as she gets out the car and soon as she opened the door O'Dell eyes zoomed toward the door and saw a pair of red and green air max, but when he saw the rest of her outfit he dropped the bucket of water and laughed as she stands there with her hands on her hips as she smiles and looks at him as he laughs and picks up the bucket.

"This what we on huh, lol."

"Ask and you shall receive, lol." Zella says as she walks toward him biting her bottom lip while laughing before giving him a hug and he grabs her ass, as she jumps and says ooh.

"So, where is my bucket at."

"You can have this one, I'll go get me another one." O'Dell says as he heads back into the garage to get another bucket as Zella sprays him with the water hose.

Sharday makes it home to see some roses on her doorstep with a card. She was shocked and surprised all at the same time, then smiles as she enters her door gets situated and puts her phone on the charger and runs her water for her coffee and her phone rings while she was in the kitchen, it was Diego.

"Hello." Sharday answers while laughing.

"Well hello stranger."

"Hello stranger my ass and if you not calling me to come ride your face, wtf are you calling me for then." Sharday says with aggression and seriousness.

"Damn that's how you feel." Diego asks.

"Yea because you been blowing me up with all the calls and messages, so I'm going to assume you want to suck this pussy, because you couldn't possibly want nothing else." Sharday says while laughing.

"Well since you put it like that, I can do that when you want to fuck my face." Diego says.

"The fuck you mean when, right now nigga so you coming right now or not." Sharday says.

"Damn so fucking aggressive, but I'm going to need like an hour." Diego says.

"I said right now, you got me fucked up, so never mind as she hangs up while Diego looks at his phone in shock and laughs as she text O'Dell.

"We still on for tonight." Sharday text O'Dell as he calls her.

"Hello." Sharday says.

"What's up gotdammit." O'Dell says.

"Shit I'm trying to see, you tell me."

"Well actually me and Zella over her at my crib about to wash our cars; you want to come join us."

"Oh really, let me guess she wearing some booty shorts and some air max."

"Damn how you know what she was wearing." O'Dell asks her as he looks around to see if she was nearby because that is exactly what she was wearing.

"Will tell you about it in a minute."

"That's what's up we here."

So after treating Diego she decides to stop by O'Dell house to join him and Zella, somewhere she doesn't have to ask to get her pussy devoured by two people at the same time, then on her way out the house Zella texted her.

"Hey boo I'm over here at O'Dell oops I mean O'Damn crib about to help him wash his car and this punk then wet me up, you should join us." Zella says.

"He already told me I'm omw as we speak, lol." Sharday says.

As soon as Sharday pulls up to see Zella bent over washing his wheels and all she sees is Zella ass, then O'Dell sprayed her with the water hose as she smiles and screams out.

"Wet that ass up baby." Sharday yells out the window as Zella starts twerking while he shoots her with the hose and Sharday parks behind Zella car and gets out wearing some red legging, orange and red balance shoes and a V-neck t-shirt with no bra. But as soon as she put her leg out the car Diego calls her, she looks at her phone and ignored it., then greets Zella with a hug, a kiss on the cheek and an ass grab.

"Where is my hug at." O'Dell says.

Sharday smiles and gives him a hug as he palms her ass with both of his hands.

"Well I see somebody miss me." Sharday says while smiling.

"Just a little. "O'Dell says as he smiles.

Sharday looks at him with the side eye.

"Yea Aight, whatever." Sharday says as her phone rings, and it was Diego thirsty ass.

"Who the fuck is that calling boo on my time." Zella asks with aggression and laughter.

"OMFG, Diego thirsty ass." Sharday says while frowning as Zella snatches her phone out of her hand.

"Let me answer it the next time he call, because I can tell the way you talk about him you tired of his shit." Zella says.

"Now hoe you might sell him a dream, I know your ass, and I don't have time for that, with his stalking ass." Sharday says while smiling.

"Now why would I do that." Zella says as she folds her arms and smirks.

"Because you have done it before, with your slick ass." Sharday says.

"Lmao ok but not this time." Zella says with the side eye.

"Yea whatever lol." Sharday says with laughter.

So, O'Dell sat there and watched them debate over who was going to answer Sharday phone, while he was thinking of a masterplan to knock both of them down....at the same time. As Zella felt him eyeballing them.

"Sharday look at this creep". Zella whispers to Sharday as they turned around and looked at him

"O'Dell what's up with that devilish look your giving us." Sharday ask him.

"I plead the fifth." O'Dell says while grinning.

"So, you telling me you wasn't over there plotting some wild and freaky shit about us." Zella ask as her and Sharday stands there smirking as they folds their arms.

"Nope...it was some wild, crazy, and freaky shit, lol." O'Dell says as he laughs as he sprays the two of them with the water hose.

"Old punk ass." Sharday says as she smiles, looks at Zella then looks at her shirt because he just sprayed.

And as soon as O'Dell turned his back and then they double teamed with his water hose and the bucket he gave Zella. He tried to run away before they ran him down, then he was left standing there wet as hell, while the two of them are laughing their ass off.

"Payback a bitch." O'Dell says while smiling and squeezing water out his shirt.

"We know that but, in the meantime, I need to get out of these wet clothes, so I'm going to go in here and steal some of O'Dell shorts and take a shower, Yall going to join me." Sharday says as she walks into the house eye balling O' Dell and winking at Zella as she goes in right after Sharday.

O'Dell laughs as Zella walks in the house behind Sharday.

"I'm Coming ladies." O'Dell says after he mumbles after yall cum, lol.

So, they headed in the house then Zella felt Sharday phone vibrate it was Flex, she showed her.

"Girl, fuck that phone he gotta wait to." Sharday says as she takes her phone from Zella and throws it on the couch then walks toward the washroom.

So, he went to get him some boxers out of his room, then he heard the shower running, he went in the washroom and saw Zella and Sharday had already started without him. Sharday was standing in the shower in front of Zella kissing her on the neck as Zella closed her eyes in pleasure leaning her head back as Sharday pulls her hair, then makes it to her twins as Zella opened her eyes to see O'Dell Standing there, she gives him the come here finger. He threw those boxers on the floor, stripped down and walked towards the shower and gets in with them and gets behind Zella and started kissing on her neck and back while taking his hand and raising her leg then grabbing Sharday head and putting it between Zella legs as Sharday begins to slowly finger Zella pussy as it gets juicy and she starts to eat her kitty for about 10 minutes then she fingers her again and after takes the two fingers and put them in Zella mouth as she sucks all of her own juices off them then she sticks her finger in her pussy again and told O'Dell your turn, and he sucked her fingers clean, then he started tongue kissing Zella as he grabs Sharday by the throat and she moaned and smiled as Zella turned Sharday around.

"OMG, this ass is nice as hell and I missed it." Zella said as she got behind Sharday, squatted down to kiss her cheeks, took her tongue, and stuck it in Sharday asshole as she jumped and start shaking it a little. The Zella raises up and takes Sharday shoulders and pushes her down to be face to face with O'Dell monster and makes her bend over so she could suck her pussy from the back while she sucks O'Dell dick, as O'Dell took his hands and spreaded Sharday ass so Zella can eat nothing but pussy. Then Sharday looked back at Zella opened her legs up a little wider and arched her back a little more then, she shoved his monster in her food hole, while getting tongue fucked from the back by Zella.

Zella had Sharday shaking and moaning with a mouth full dick. And she was coming so hard from Zella eating her pussy he grabbed her head with both his hands and made his monster fit all the way in her mouth, as he started to fuck her mouth before she stopped him and took his dick out her mouth.

"OMG Zella I'm about to cum baby." Sharday says as she takes her hand and grabs Zella head as Zella starts doing tongue exercises on Sharday, as she came all in Zella mouth and she sucked her pussy the whole she was coming as O'Dell was fucking her mouth. The three of them needed a real session because that shower was not enough space to perform properly.

"Wheeew, Aw hell naw bring yall ass to this room." Sharday says as she gets out shower and heads to bedroom.

"Zella you a beast, no lie." O'Dell says to her while smiling.

"Hey yo dick game crazy boy stop playing." Zella says to him as she looks at his dick, kisses it and gets out the shower and heads to the room where Sharday is waiting. O'Dell makes it to the room to see them kissing.

"Bring that pussy here." O'Dell says as he lays on the bedroom floor.

Zella and Sharday looks at each other, smiles and walks over to where he was laying on the floor at, Sharday walks over and stands over his face, He sticks his tongue out, she squats on that thick motherfukker and rode his tongue, while Zella came over and begin to eat his dick, for a little while until it rises to the occasion, the she sits on it, but it was so hard by the time she sat all the way down on it and he started fucking her…

"Oh, shit daddy I'm about to cum, shit, fuck, gotdammit." Zella says as she bounces on his dick three times then, she starts to cover his member with her creams as Sharday grabs her titties.

"Oh, shit me to, yesssss daddy get that cream." Sharday says as he looks at Zella as she bounces on his dick and her cream is splashing everywhere, then Sharday hears her phone ringing again…it was Flex. She couldn't make it to answer, then he sent two messages. Meanwhile, Sharday talked shit, rode his fact, and talked more shit and straddled his tongue more until she came three times. Then she got up from off his face and watched Zella as she turned around switch positions and was fucking the shit out of him. Because the last orgasm she had he had her shaking like she was having a seizure, screaming, and shaking. She was about to cum again and tried to get up to avoid giving him the upper hand sexually, but he was not going as soon as she tried to get up and runaway he grabbed her waist and was bouncing her on that monster as she screamed while Coming screaming his name, and after that nut she went to ride his face, as Sharday stood by the sink in the bathroom laughing and smiling. So, after twenty minutes of him eating Zella pussy he stopped.

"Hey you." O'Dell says while giving Sharday the come here finger as he smacks on Zella pussy as he points to his rock-solid member, as Sharday laughs.

"Yall not about to make me tap out tonight." O'Dell says as he takes Zella pussy out his mouth and stands up and lets Zella get his dick nice and wet for

Sharday to receive it. Sharday turned around looked at how hard his dick was, and she got on her knees and bent over with ease. As Zella licked her pussy a couple times, then stuck O'Dell dick in her mouth to get it wet before putting it in Sharday pussy as she growls and shakes her legs as Zella went to lay on the floor in front of her.

"Stfu and take that dick and suck on this pussy, bitch." Zella says to Sharday as she kisses her then lays on the floor as Sharday gets on her knees to eat her pussy while he fucks her from the back, for about thirty minutes until he was about to cum.

"Oooh shit ladies I'm about to bust, and this a big one." O'Dell says as he pulls out of Sharday pussy and stands over the two of them and lets them share the nut between their faces, and when he finished getting his nut out Sharday grabbed his dick to drain it bone dry as Zella sucks and squeezes is balls to make sure they got every drop out of him.

They fukked in the shower and then got to the bedroom and fukked some more. Now it's a little pass 2 a.m. And O'Dell got payback from the last time the three of them linked up. The three of them stayed in the shower for like an hour pleasing each other beyond measures and making each other have several orgasms they finally finished and headed to the bedroom to go lay down. As, each one of them actually went to take a shower individually to actually clean up and shower as O'Dell went downstairs to shower in the other washroom., as Zella goes in after Sharday comes out. Sharday gets out the shower, heard her phone ring and she grabs her phone so she can call Flex back. After 15 minutes passed Zella gets out the shower and goes in the room to talk to Sharday as she was sitting on the bed with the lotion on the bed next to her before falling asleep.

Chapter 3: Pleasured Fun

So, the next morning, Zella and Sharday woke up finishing the conversation they was having earlier yesterday after the both of them got out the shower.

"So, you going to call your boy back, because you a popular little hoe." Zella ask Sharday as she got out the shower and was drying off.

"Shut up bitch." Sharday says as she starts to put on her lotion.

"Ijs what do buddy Diego be on."

"He Just a bug, with a weak ass dick game, but a raw ass head game." Sharday says as she stands up and put lotion on her legs.

"Let me put that on them sexy legs baby."

"Thanks boo."

"He cool but he be doing too much but don't do enough, if you know what I mean."

"Aw I totally feel where you coming from, I will be right back." Zella says to Sharday as she goes downstairs to check on O'Dell be it was so quiet.

"Lmao, what the hell". Zella while walking back upstairs.

"Good job boo." Zella says to Sharday as she gives her a high five.

"What was that for and what happened."

"That nigga still down their sleep with the dry towel still on." Zella says as she laughs.

So, it's about 8 a.m. Sharday phone started ringing as soon as she came back in from getting her hoe bag out the car.

It was Flex calling her; she answered at the same time O'Dell came upstairs and got in that bed and laid back down. You see O'Dell and Sharday have an understanding, my time is my time and jealously is not tolerated.

"What's happening boss lady." Flex says to Sharday as she puts on her panties and Zella straps up her bra for her.

"Thanks boo, and shit putting on my clothes, what you up to." Sharday says as she smiles.

"Shit what you doing later today."

"Nothing but lunch with my girlfriend, why what's up."

"Trying to see if your available."

"I think I can make that happen, around what time you talking about." Sharday says while as she puts on her sweats up ties up her shoes. While watching Zella bending over putting while was putting on her pants then give her ass a slap

"Four should be good, if that works for you."

"Ok I'm going to hit you around 3:30 to confirm." Sharday says as Zella whispers is that Flex and she replies yes.

"Hey Flex." Zella screams with a big ass smile as she walks pass and smacks Sharday on the ass and she jumps on the bed while O'Dell was laying down and hits him with the pillows.

"What's happening bad, bad." Flex speaks to Zella as he smirks.

"Get...yo...punk...ass... up...nigga." Zella says while hitting O'Dell with pillow as he laid in the bed.

"Well go ahead and finish up what you have going on I will keep you posted." Flex says to Sharday as O'Dell get up and grabs Zella and slams her on the bed, stands up in the bed as his towel hangs on his man meat because all that physical pillow abuse got him aroused, Zella looked at Sharday as the both of them looked at the towel hanging like a coat on a coat rack then looked at O'Dell as he smiles.

"Ya'll crazy." O'Dell says as he walks away to go get his clothes out closet.

"So, when I got out the shower and came downstairs, I seen yo ass in the bed knocked out sleep, lol." Zella says while smiling.

"Fuck you and mother fuck her." O'Dell says to Zella while pointing to Sharday.

Zella looked at Sharday and smiled

"Is that another challenge I hear." Sharday laughs at him while looking at Zella.

"Sounds like it to me." Zella says as she puts her hands on her hips.

"Be careful now because I never back down from a challenge, or two. And for the record I might tap out, but I guarantee both of yall I can go for more right now." O'Dell says as he stand up stretches and heads to closet to look for a shirt.

"Whatever dude." Sharday says while laughing.

"Not to mention neither one of ya'll have ever fukked with a nigga that can handle both of yall together, at the same time." O'Dell says as he puts his shirt on.

Sharday grins and looks at Zella and smiles

"Well he does have a point Zella." Sharday says as he smiles at Zella.

"Yes, I second that because your name speaks for itself." Zella says as the both of them yell "O'Damn" at the same time in a sexual way as he smiles.

"Fukking Punks." O'Damn says as he watched them laughing as they walked out the room heading downstairs.

"Ok O'Dell we about to head out." Zella says to him.

"We going to talk to you later." Sharday yells from the front door as he walks up front to see her off properly.

"Ok bring it in." O'Dell says in as he gets a hug and kiss from Zella and grabbed her ass, as she smiled and jumped and slapped him on the ass. And then he got a hug and kiss from Sharday as he grabbed her ass, and she grabbed his dick as he smiled.

"Until next time." Sharday says to him smiling.

"You already know it." O'Dell says as he watches those two nice asses walk away as he closes the door smiling.

Walking to her car Sharday calls Zack back.

"What's happening gotdammit." Zack answers.

"Chilling what you been up to punk." Sharday ask him as Zella smiles as she hears her call him a punk.

"Shit working and living life, what you been up too lil freaky."

Sharday laughs because of what they did yesterday, and it gave her shivers, chill bumps and made her moist just thinking about his touch.

"That be you Mr. come sit on my face baby." Sharday says while laughing.

"Ijs you talking like you want to come do it right now or something, lol." Zack says while laughing.

As Sharday gets quiet and smiles.

'Maybe."

"Aw shit I know what your maybe mean."

Sharday laughs loud as hell.

"And what may that be."

"Maybe you want to sit on my face, maybe you want to fukk my face, or maybe you just want to stroke my tongue, while fukking my face lol." Zack says as he laughs.

Sharday giggles, laughs and smiles

"Or maybe I want to do all of that and some." Sharday says.

"Well Maybe you need to give me a time and location because as long as I have a face you will always have a place to sit, lol."

"Well I'm kind of busy right now but I got you on speed dial, so give me a second I'm going to keep you posted if anything changes.

"Aight ttyl."

"Yup, Yup." Sharday says then she gets a message soon as she hung up. She looks at the message with the curious look, and she looks at it again when she pulls up to her driveway.

Sharday makes it home and sits in the car plotting on Flex since she already got Zack and O'Dell out the way, and now she wants some head from Diego. Then she came up with a plan that was kind of freaky, devious, exciting, spontaneous, and awesome. Then O'Dell text her while she was getting out the car.

"Hey quitter wyd, lol." O'Damn says.

"Wait, you talking shit now." Sharday ask him.

"Quit playing you already know I talk shit all day because I can back it up."

"But I got the power so your shit talking can be overpowered by this pussy if you don't already know."

"So, what you saying Sharday you challenging me."

"Ok fukk it, you can't make me tap out and I can't be defeated, by you I might say O damn a million times but that doesn't mean you won, so wassup now." Sharday says.

"Oh really, can't be defeated, you funny as hell. Ok since we are both 2-2 here is the bet who ever taps out has to do any three favors the winner ask." O'Damn says.

"Wait anything."

"Anything and I mean anything, nothing is off limits." O'Damn says while laughing.

"Aight I will take that bet, so when this supposed to take place."

"In 48 hours so clear your schedule cause It's on."

"Lmao aight bet you on but let me get my other line I'm going to hit you back in a minute."

"Aight cool."

Zack was feeling some kind of way, so he texted Sharday.

"Call me when you get a chance."

"Hello." Zack says.

"What's happening, you good." Sharday says

"Can I ask you a Question."

"Sure, what's up."

"If you was fucking someone other than me, would you tell me."

Sharday laughs and giggles.

"If you asked me, but why would it matter anyway." Sharday says while giggling.

"So, wait I have to ask you."

"Yea, because if you really want to know then you would ask, just like if I really wanted you to know then I would tell you."

Zack smiles, laughs, and giggles.

"Aw ok cool, so we still on for later."

"So far so good."

"Ok I will see you later."

So, once Zella gets situated in her car, she calls Sharday and they were talking about who Sharday should take down tonight, then Zella started asking sex related questions and Sharday began answering.

"So, I have several invites to come out and have an awesome time, and I don't know who to take up on their offer.

"Oh really, was it threatening." Zella says while giggling.

"Naw silly."

"Aw I was about to say don't threatening me with a good time, but who are the lucky guys to choose from." Zella asks while laughing.

"Zack and Flex but Diego is trying to get a hold of me too, because you know he trying to redeem his self from the last time."

"Decisions, decisions, I got a question which one of these guys are the best when they are at their best?" Zella asks her as she giggles

"You see Zack is better at one thing, but Flex is a mixture of both and a true gentleman, and Diego just gives great head, lol. "Sharday says while smiling.

"Damn great head, what about his dick game." Zella asks.

Sharday changes the subject.

"Anyway, But I must say no one can compare to O'Dell, Lol but Flex is the closet one to perfect because he is a thuggish sweetheart."

"So, what are you plans and what about Diego."

"I'm going to have some fun and Diego is going to get sent off after he suck this pussy and eat this ass lmao."

"Sounds like you are going to choose Flex because thuggish sweethearts know how to have fun." Zella says while laughing.

"You already know, and I'm not counting O'Dell out just yet and Diego can be useful to."

"So just hit me in a minute with the sexual update, lol." Zella says while laughing and remembering that she never mentioned to Sharday that Zack was coming over mom house for dinner, but it didn't really matter because she never told her that she was still fucking him either, so she didn't feel bad.

Chapter 4- Who's Next

So, it was Flex texting her asking her was she ready for him. So Sharday never replied to Flex Message because she still trying to put together her plan, but he texted back never mind, you ain't ready. Now he knows she loves and hates shit talkers because she love it when they talk shit, but hate it when they can't back it up, but flex can back up all the shit he talks. So, he called her bluff, and she didn't bite that time, but he texted her again and said whenever you ready and think you can handle all this Dick hit me up. She was about to reply to the last message when that one came through. But she let him get the last laugh, and she did not reply.

First of all, why in the hell is Diego always trying to get some pussy knowing he can't handle it, even though he has great head, sometimes I need some dick to follow up great head, lol. Second, why is Zack getting all mushy about what she does in her free time away from him? it's not like they're together, although he is the closet to being her guy if her having a man was the plan. Third, why is O'Damn such a damn dawg but one of the best fucks she has ever had, in her life more like the best, lol. and Fourth, what is flex up to because he been doing a lot lately as far as everything being a friend, fuck buddy, companion and homey and not looking for relationship. So now she becomes really about what is flex up to, so she calls her homegirl to see if she could give her an idea of what these men are up too but first she wanted to talk to flex about all the guys cause he knows about all of them and doesn't care as long as his time is his time.

Sharday calls flex.

"What up buddy." Sharday says as she giggles.

"What's happening." Flex says.

"I want to talk to you about something and I want your honest opinion."

"Ok cool I can do that so is this going to happen in person or over the phone."

"In person."

"Aw ok, My place or yours."

"Yours, I'm omw."

"Ok cool."

So Sharday is driving to Flex house and her juices were flowing thinking about her last encounter with him. And it was so bad she sat at the red light, closed her eyes and starting biting her lip from the thought of him fukking her. Then she felt her phone vibrate opened her eyes and the light was green, and she looked at her phone on her lap, she noticed she had got wet again.

"These men are something else shiiiit." Sharday says.

Then O'Damn sends Sharday a picture of his dick.

"He just asked about you." O'Damn says with smiley emojis

So, she decides to use Flex as a test run for this competition with O Damn. Because she has something, she has always wanted him to do so she is claiming the victory already. Sharday is heading to Flex house that dick on the brain and receives a call from Zella soon as she parks.

"What up hoe." Sharday says as she answers the phone.

"Wyd." Zella asks.

"About to go and jump on a dick u good."

"Oh yea, wait who dick you about to ride, now."

"Flex, because he been talking the most shit, plus I need to use him anyway, lol." Sharday says as she laughs.

"Well go ahead and bust one, I mean two because he might have that thunder dick." Zella says while smiling.

"Idk, because I don't put nothing pass his ass." Sharday says as she laughs.

"Lol, yesssss, baby you alright because sounds like u got something on your mind."

"I do but, I'll just ttyl about it, because it's kind of a lot."

"Ok sweetheart, well we will talk about it later." Zella says as she hangs up, then calls Zack.

"What's up buddy, wyd." Zella asks.

"What's happening punk." Zack says.

"Was about to head home but I'm just curious, wyd later on."

"Shit chilling what's up."

"Mom asked about you wanted to know if you wanted to come over for dinner tonight." Zella asked him.

"I will try but I am kinda tired." Zack says as he yawns.

"Well just so you know she cooking your favorite." Zella says as she laughs.

"Corn beef, cabbage, macaroni & cheese and hot water cornbread." He says.

"You already know it." Zella says.

'Oh, hell yea I will sleep better after that meal anyway, lol, what time." Zack asks.

"Around seven at moms house." Zella says.

"Ok see yall at seven." Zack says.

"Ok I will let them know you coming to dinner."

"No don't tell them I want it to be a surprise."

"Ok cool."

Shortly after Zella and Sharday was talking. Diego texted Sharday one time, Zack texted her once, O'Dell texted her once and sent one picture message. And one text from Flex

After reading messages she called Flex, and whatever he said it got her worked up in other words, she got wet, then she decided to open up one of O'Dell messages and it was a dick pic she got wet even more.

"Flex yo ass still talking shit." Sharday says to herself as she laughs.

"Yo ass is mine, so prepare to do whatever I have in mind." Flex replies.

"You really on one huh lil buddy, we will see." Sharday says.

Sharday laughs at Flex text, as she read Zack text.

"We can meet up but I'm horny ass shit, and I'm going to need a rematch because I felt like you took advantage of me, LOL." Zack says.

"You play games to many games, but that pussy taste so fukking good." Diego says with smiley face emojis as she laughs.

"Hope you ready to tap out because your ass is well overdue, LOL." O'Dell says.

Sharday laughs at all the messages and says my oh, as Zack makes it over to Zella mom house for dinner.

You see Zack and Zella's brother was best friends before he went to jail. And while he was away Zella and Zack stayed in touch, they even became closer because he was still coming around the family even though her brother wasn't there. Then Zack moved away from like a year but moved back home. You see Zella always had a crush on him, but she never told him and that's when he started having feelings for Sharday. Because they was young and Sharday was a wildcat and Zella was the quiet type, plus her brother was not having them dating. But over time Sharday started gaining feelings for Zack as well, but she doesn't want a relationship and she thinks that's what he wants, but she is in for a surprise.

So, mom greeted Zack at the door with a big hug.

"Hey, Zack how have you been we really missed you. We was starting to get worried." Mom says after she hugs him and looks at him

"I been around." Zack says as he looks at Zella and laughs.

"You want to say grace Zack." Mom asks as everyone sits down for dinner.

"Ok that's fine."

"Zella no Sharday tonight." Mom asked as she brings the steaming hot cornbread to the table and sits down.

"Naw when I talked to her earlier, she said she had something to do."

"Now is that the truth or did you even tell her I was cooking." Mom asks her as she gives her the mom look.

"No, I didn't tell her because she had already told me she had something to take care of."

"Oh, really or is Zack being here the real reason you didn't tell her, and despite of what she had to do you still should have extended the invitation." Mom says as Zella smirked and put her head down, then grinned lifted her head and laughed.

"No disrespect mom, but I had nothing to do with Sharday not being here."

"I know Zack that's all Zella, but you did have something to do with her not being here." Mom says as the table got quiet as hell.

"Anyway, can you pass me the Macaroni & cheese Zella." Mom says as she looks at the two of them and smiles.

Then Zack gets a text from Sharday, he looks at his phone and smirks.

"What's up boo you busy."

Then she texted Zella

"Bitch we need to talk, asap."

"Aight hoe give me a minute," Zella says. Then Sharday phone blows up. She received two messages from Diego, two from Flex, and one from O'Dell.

So, they finish eating dinner and Zella and Zack cleaned up the kitchen then left the table and went down to the basement to chillout. As they was talking about old times, the wine began to hit Zella and she started to speak her mind. Then Sharday text Zella again.

"You know what imma call Diego bluff, I want to see if the head still the same or better." Sharday text Zella.

Sharday calls Diego, and he picks up on the first ring.

"Hello."

"What's up mister, you ready to stop playing with me."

"You funny as hell and you tell me, since I have to stalk yo ass." Diego says while laughing.

"Naw I just been busy but, what's up with all this shit talking u been doing lately, last time we talked I had to treat yo ass because you was acting like you didn't know what it was.

"Whatever quit playing hard to get and come holla at me, so I can make that pussy cry." Diego says while laughing.

"Ok well damn since you want to do that, when." Sharday asks.

"Whenever you ready to run and leak, yo call." Diego says.

Oh, really other line clicks its O'Damn, but she sends him a message that he will call him back.

"So now back to these freaky gestures you been making about me." Sharday says.

"They're not gestures because you need to quit playing and let me suck on that pussy." Diego says.

"Well damn, ok well imma hit you when I'm on my way." Sharday says.

"Do that and don't stand me up motherfukker because you'll only make the oral punishment worst." Diego says as he giggles.

"Don't threaten me with a good time." Sharday says as she laughs

"Ok see you in a minute."

"Yup, Yup." Sharday says as she hangs up.

She was on her way to Flex house and was still texting Diego, and continues to message Flex, then pulls over and sits and thinks to herself. If should she let Diego taste her or just try to take O'Damn in this challenge but she does like Diego mouthpiece, so she accepts Diego invitation detours and heads over to Diego house, but little did she know, she's in for a rude awakening from him because she always stands him up for one, and for two he's out to kill that pussy one way or another. Meanwhile, Zella has a way of saying things when she gets tipsy and Zack has a way of responding back to tipsy women and she knows this plus she has no filter when she feeling herself, and she says somethings and Zack responses fukked her up.

So Sharday makes her way over to Diego house, he sees her pulling up and he opens door for her as she approaches as he smiles.

"I guess you wasn't scared after all." Diego says as he smiles, and she looked at him and laughed.

"Scared boy whatever, hopefully, you can back up all that shit talking cause your 0-3 so far buddy." Sharday says as she pushed him out the way and forced her way in the house. Then Sharday pulls her phone out and puts it on vibrate.

"I don't think you ready for me, because the last couple times you been losing to This pussy, lol."

"Well that's because you never gave me a chance to introduce myself plus your always in a hurry or rush so if you have time and don't be surprised at the sounds, noises and reactions you give off from what I'm going to do to that pussy." Diego Says as he laughs.

She looked at him and laughed. So, she goes in the living room and gets comfortable sits down and they start to talk as he heads to grab some coolers out the fridge and comes back in the living room and hands her one.

"So, what you mean I been lately losing to that pussy." Diego ask her.

"Exactly what I said this pussy been getting the best of you and I'm starting to believe that we are too much for you to handle." Sharday as she opens up her cooler.

"We." Diego laughs

"Yea nigga me and her." Sharday says as she points to her pussy.

"You really feeling yourself huh, LOL."

"I'm actually not but this Juicebox is dangerous and I think you know that." Sharday says as she walks over towards him kicks off her shoes and plants her foot on his thigh looks at him, smiles.

"You're not going to stop until I make you tap out, I see and literally punish that pussy, because you keep fucking with me."

"Nope cause for one, you can't make me tap out, and two I'm never going to stop because I can hang with the best of them and you have yet to prove me that you're a big dawg. Sharday says as she smiles.

Then Diego grabs her by the thigh flips her over, as she smiles and lays there.

"Well let's find out. As he starts to kiss her inner thigh and looks at her while he was doing it. Sharday jumps and says oooh I like that as she bites her finger.

"What you got up your sleeve."

"Whatever it is you are going to like it." Diego says as he kisses her other inner thigh as Sharday starts to massage his shoulders as he sucks on her thighs while he unbuttons her shorts with the left hand. As he continue to kiss her other leg as she raises both of her legs as he pulls the shorts down with the right hand as she smiles, and juices started to flow. Meanwhile Zella and Zack are chilling in the basement when out of nowhere Zella the liquor kicks in and Zack notices it quick.

"Zack, I have a question."

"Zella, I have the answer.

"Naw but what's up." Zack asks as he grabs the bottle of tequila off the table.

"What would you say if I told you in use to had a crush on you when we was younger."

"I would say how come you never told me." Zack says as he grabs her cup to pour her a shot.

"Because I didn't think you felt the same way or was even into me like that."

"How would you know, how I felt about you if you never even bothered to tell me how you felt, because you never know how I felt about you, I could have felt the same way." Zack says as he stares at her with the evil eye as he sips his drink.

Zella looks in shock and replies

"But you never showed any signs that you were."

"And I never showed you I wasn't, and your horrible at seeing the signs because I actually did show you several times, that I was interested in you." Zack says while dropping ice cubes in her drink as he sips his drink and laughs.

Zella laughs, sips her wine, and laughs

"So, you saying you don't like me anymore." Zack says as he grabs brings drink and moves closer to her as she smiles.

"I mean." Zella says as she sips her drink and smiles as Zack interrupts her statement, then kisses her slowly and romantically as she became so into his passionate kisses, she grabbed his face and continues to kiss him back. Zack stopped kissing Zella and looked at her. As she opened her eyes to see zack looking at her smiling.

She moves back in her seat and sits there with the look of shock on her face.

"Wow.'

"What's the matter, everything ok."

"Nothing I just never would have never imagined years ago that you would give me the warm feeling in my soul from a kiss." Zella says as he looks shocked.

"Warm feeling." Zack says as he smiles as he sits with the biggest grin on his face.

"Yes, that kiss just did something to me that I can't even find the words to explain what it actually was."

"And I always use to think if your lips were as soft as they looked." Zack says as he moved closer to her and kissed her again as she gave him one in return while grabbing his face.

Meanwhile, soon as Diego pulls down Sharday shorts he sees the camel toe. She opened her legs up and all Diego heard was the macaroni sound. Diego looked at Sharday she was smiling as, he grinned as she bit her finger as he began his taste test he slowly licked three times and watched juices flow as the fourth lick as catches them with his quick tongue, then he begin to tongue fukk her, her toes slightly curled, as she made a fist with both of her hands. While he sucked her pussy while she was balling up her fist, then she released her fingers to grab his head, then she let go. As he went deeper.

"Stop playing with me, and grab my head with both of your hands, gotdammit." Diego says. As she did just that and smiled while he was working doing it as he raised her ass up with both of his hands, licked her ass and made his way back to her pussy, and sucked on her clit as she shook slowly.

"Oooh…. shit." Sharday says as she almost came but she held it back, as she threw her head back.

Now Zack has made Zella pussy juicy.

"Whew." Zella says as she sits back and clinches her legs closed as he looked at her.

"What was all that for."

"Those kisses just got made my monkey semi-leaky, what the fukk." Zella says as he laughed.

Zack smile and giggles.

"No for real I love that kinda shit, it just does something to me."

"I can tell."

"Whatever nigga how can you tell."

"Because your nipples are hard ass shit." Zack says as Zella feels her boobs, and they are she looks down at them and smiles.

"Oh damn, I'm trying to tell you, don't start nothing you can't finish."

"Well better believe if I start it, I plan on finishing it." Zack says as he smiles and gets closer.

"Is that so." Zella says as she leans back as he gets closer.

"Yes, Yes."

Meanwhile Diego started doing tongue exercises on Sharday so good she squirted three times in 15 minutes.

"Gottttttttt damnnn nigga what the fukk you doing down there, shit." Sharday says as she grabs his head from the back to controlling the motion...he moves hands.

"Be cool baby let me work." Diego says as he takes control.

Then he takes her hands and tell her to place them right under her lower back to make that pussy sit up. And she does just that, then he spreads her legs and grabs her calves...

Then Diego dives in tongue first, sucks on that thang while she was shaking her life away as she moans, creams, shakes, and screams as she moans.

"Oooh baby eat it, eat it, oh shit I'm Cumming again, fuuuuck, seconds after as he rapidly gives her clit a tongue exercise, she screams out shiiiit I'm Cumming again baby. While shaking, then she begin to squirt as he starts to finger her to make her squirt more, as she grabs the top of the couch and squirts more. He stops as she wipes sweat, then he flipped her over and told her to spread that motherfukker wide open she replied yes daddy and grabs her cheeks and spreads that ass just like he told her to.

Meanwhile on the other side of town, Zack moves closer to Zella and squeezes her boobs.

"Damn they are as soft as I imagined." Zack says as he looked at Zella and smiled.

"You going to keep on playing with me huh."

"Maybe." Zack says as he gives her that look and takes his hand and puts it down her pants to feel the wet, wet, pulls it out and then sucks his finger.

Zella giggled and smiled.

"Damn it even taste good."

Zella sits there with this look on her face as he removed his hand, as her mother opened the door at the top of the stairs.

"Yall ok down there." mom says out of curiosity.

"Yea was just finishing up the rest of this wine, before heading back to the store, did you want something back?

"No, I'm good." Mom says.

"Ok we will be right back, were going to go out the back door."

As her and Zack get up and go to the store and as soon as they get in the car, she grabs his dick.

"I'm going to need some of this tonight." Zella says as she grabs his dick.

"Ok let's make it happen." Zack says as he smiles.

So, Zella and Zack drove to the store to get more drinks and headed back to the house. Zella goes upstairs to see everyone is sleep, goes back downstairs, looked at Zack grabs his hand, and headed to the room to get what she has been wanting for, for the longest.

Sharday grabs her cheeks and spread them, just like Diego told her then he takes his dick and inserts the head in slowly as Sharday shivers shakes jumps and says. Yesssss then he puts it all the way in she shouts.

"Fuuuuck, Yesssss, Baby." Sharday screams as he slow strokes her till she starts to fuck him back, and he defended himself better this time because he grabbed her waist and threw that dick all up in her guts as she was fucking him back.

Soon as Zella closed the upstairs door, she went downstairs then her and Zack started kissing and undressing each other, then her mom opened the door.

"Zella is that you." Mom asks.

"Yea it's me mom", while putting her shirt back on because she thought she was coming down there.

Meanwhile Diego gets ten strokes in, she had his dick looking like a ice cream cone.

"Omfg, gotdammit what's got into you Diego." Sharday says as she watches him pound her box while she bites her lip.

"Stfu and spread that ass, bitch." Diego says as she looks shocked, smiled and did just that as she planted her face n the couch.

As he pounded.... and....pounded.

"OMFG." Sharday says as she squirted everywhere.

As Diego smiles as he beats her box up even more

"While Sharday was moaning fukk me daddy.... he pounded more and she milked him more.

Then Sharday receives a text from O'Damn but she was too busy to answer.

Chapter 5 – Only the strong survive

Sharday came about eight times before she fell down and laid out on the couch for ten minutes, jumped up and said ok my turn. Grabbed Diego pushed him down.

"Lay yo ass down boy and put your seatbelt on buddy lol." Sharday says as she gets up and Diego smiles at her.

Zella buttons last button up while

"You can come in mom." Zella says to mom.

Mom peeks her head when she makes it near the bottom and looks around being nosey.

"Yall ok down here."

"Yea just sitting here talking and having a drink, you want a glass."

"That's ok I took meds earlier; Zack are you staying the night."

He looks at Zella and smiles.

"Not sure yet mama, kind of hard to decide right now."

"Nigga I'm not putting a gun to your head and making you drink it lmao."

"Seems like it the way you keep saying turn up nigga lmao." Zack says while laughing. As Zella acts like she about to hit him

"Well Goodnight yall, I'm going back to bed, see yall in the morning." Mom says as she walks back upstairs laughing.

"Goodnight mom." Zella says.

"Goodnight." Zack says.

Mom gives Zella this look and she closed the door, as Zack moves is hand so mom wouldn't see his pants were unbuckled.

"You think she on to you." Zack asked Zella.

"Nah she half sleep, Now where was I as she leaned over kissed Zack and straddled him. Zella started kissing Zack as he put his hand under the back of her shirt and unstrapped her bra with one hand and grabbed a hand full ass with the other, then Zella hit the remote-control light and turned it off.

Meanwhile, Sharday heard her phone vibrate again, she paid it no mind as she sucked her juices off of Diego dick, licked up his shaft sucked, slobbed and spit all on his dick, then took all his man meat to the back Of her throat, gagged swallowed her spit, kept going and pulled it out, slightly bites the head, spits on it before slurping all the slob up, right before she sat on it and slow stroked the fukk out of him for about seven strokes before.

"Oh shit, I'm about to cum." Diego says as she jumps off of him and eats the dick and says no, no, no, not now he laughs as she gags on it stops his nut and jumps back on it.... he says O'Damn as she smiled.

On the other side of town. Zack took his hand that was on Zella ass and slide it to the front and unbuckled her pants and started fingering that pussy.

Zella flinched and said ooohhh soon as he entered, he stroked her pussy about seven or eight times before taking his finger and sucking on it again. She looked, smiled, then kissed him as he pulled her pants down slowly she stood up to remove them from her ankles, immediately after she took her pants off she pull his jogging pants and boxers down after and saw his package.

"Oh, my no wonder Sharday can't get enough off yo ass." Zella says as he laughed stood up and his dick dropped slightly her eyes dropped again.

"Well damn there's more, oh he'll yea." She says as she squatted down and introduced herself."

Meanwhile as soon as Sharday sat down on Diego dick as he closed his eyes and said mmm, mmm, mmm, damn O damn, Sharday heard that, laughed, smiled, and grinned then continued to throw that pussy.

"You going to make me bust, baby shiiiit."

"Shut the fuck up and give me that nut nigga." Sharday says as she threw it even harder.

"Fuuuck, shiiit."

"Stop holding back punk and let me get that. "Sharday says as he looked up then through his head back.

"Oh, shit hear it comes." Diego says as Sharday jumps off his dick and grabs it and started devouring it until she caught the whole load, then she squeezed his balls to get all of it.

"Wtf, omfg." Diego says as she kept sucking and five minutes later it got right back up and she jumped back on it, reversed cowgirl and said hold my hands, as he grabbed them and boy o boy, she murdered that dick.

"That was for all that shit talking you been doing." Sharday says while she was slow stroking on his member.

"WTF." Diego says.

"And this is for the shit you might want to say in the future she pulled her hands away from him, squatted got on her tip toes and started bouncing on it with no hands Diego laughed.

"Damn, fukk, shit, omfg. Diego says as he watched that ass bounce up, down, up, down, up, paused then dropped it down, rolled on it and sat down and grinded on it while watching his toes throw up gang signs, as she laughed then continued to throw it up down again then sat there.

"Oh, shit here it comes." Diego says as Sharday gave three more bounces and jumped up.

"Oooh." Diego says as he cums while she jerked his nut out until he was weak in the knees and lays on the floor from exhaustion, as Sharday looks at him and laughs.

Meanwhile, Zella was sucking on Zack so good his knees got weak.

Zella has no gag reflex, and he was shocked, when she took all of him down without even taking a breather, then she sucked on his balls while she stroked his dick, Zack looks down in shock.

"Yesssss. "Zack says as his knees buckle again, she smiles with a mouth full of dick.

Meanwhile Zella removes the dick and a slob strings trails along her lip, she slurps it up as he looks shocks as she keep going.

Then Sharday phone rings, it was Flex she didn't answer so he sent her a message, then O'Dell text her. But No call or text from Zack.

Zack is shocked at Zella performance.

So, with two hands full of hair. Zack is controlling her head as she follows while grabbing his ass and shoving his dick further and further in her mouth, as he responds.

"Hell yea, eat this dick you slut." Zack says as she grabs his ass and puts her lips all the way to his thighs and takes the whole dick as he grabs her head at the same time, and lets a load go while saying, aahh., She continue sucking and swallows every drop and keeps going as his dick gets back hard after that load as she gets up and looks at him as he sticks out his tongue as she sits on his face.

It's now 1:36 am and Sharday: The Sex Assassin was victorious again because she drained Diego dick bone dry and it's limp as hell with no chance of return she watched him sit there then she cleaned up, locked up and left him and his limp dick .On her way to her car she checked her phone, but was surprised no calls from Zack at all. So, she texted him you woke. Zack hears his phone but was super busy, so he couldn't answer.

Zella busted three nuts while riding Zack face and right after the 3rd one he grabbed her ass cheeks and was bouncing her on his tongue as she moaned "Yes daddy eat it, eat it, fuuuuck, I'm about to cum baby, as she laid her hands on his chest while bouncing on his tongue, she moans.

"I want that dick."

"Take it then." Zack says while she gets up as he licks all her juices off his lips and she jumps on his dick slowly because it's too much to force it all at once.

After Zack didn't reply Sharday returned Flex message.

"What's happening." Sharday says.

"Stranger danger what's good.' Flex says.

"Shit chilling wyd."

"Just woke up on some hungry shit."

"Oh yea, you going to cook something."

"Hell, naw about to make me a sandwich and go back to sleep, unless you going to stop by."

" Idk, you might be trying to take my goodies." Sharday says as she laughs.

"It's not taking if you give it to me."

"Whatever I'll be there in 15 min."

"Cool just call me when u close, I should be woke."

"Ok cool."

So, Sharday cleans up and heads out of Diego house, as he snores, and she laughs.

Sharday opens up the video message from O'Damn, and she was shocked as hell.

Zella moans soon as she sits down on Zack's dick as she holds her breath until she gets all of it in.

"OMFG, wtf Zack I feel this shit in my stomach damn."

"I know I feel yo insides, now stfu and take dis dick."

As Zack grabs, he waist she holds her hands over her face.

"Lord Jesus help me, LOL." Zella says as he laughs.

"The devil is a lie, as she gets all the way down, he slowly starts fucking her while she on top.

"yesssss baby, oh shit, oh shit, fukk, I'm Coming." Zella says as he keeps pounding while she creams and screams.

Then Sharday text Zella

"Girl this video O Damn just sent me, omg." Sharday says while sending smiling emojis, then Sharday text flex.

"I'm five minutes away you still woke." Sharday says.

"Ok and yea." Flex replies.

Zella had her juices all over his dick and balls but that didn't stop him from constantly beating that than up some more. Then he grabbed her neck and that made her pussy juicer than ever, then she started fukking him back as he had one hand on her neck and the other one, on her waist.

"Yea nigga give me that man meat, gotdammit." Zella says While throwing nothing but pussy on his monster.

Sharday finally makes it to Flex house as he greets her with smiles

"So, you made it."

"Yea but you know what I just want to lay down, because I have a headache and I'm kind of tired." Sharday says because she horny but tired at the same time.

"That's cool," As she takes a shower then goes to lay down."

"Ok cool, thanks again." Sharday says to Flex as she heads to the bedroom and he goes in the kitchen to get something to drink before heading to the room where she was laying down at.

"Aw now that pussy want to fight back huh.' Zack says as he picks her up flips her over and grabs her legs and stands up while holding Zella, and grabs ass and slams her on that. She moans her lungs out, fuuuck while shaking and coming. She came three times while he was holding her up.

Then Zack notices Zella sweating her ass off.

"Naw boo I'm going to need some more sweat, I'm about to make that pussy cry."

Zack says as he picks her up and carries her around the room while fucking her brains out.

Sharday slept great and when she woke up the aroma of breakfast was in the air. She rolled over Flex wasn't in the bed but then she heard her phone vibrated three times she looked at it. Diego texting her.

"You want to get breakfast." Diego says as she smiles.

O'Damn texted her Sharday.

"Can I have you for breakfast." O'Dell says as she smiled, and she put her phone down turned the volume up and went into the kitchen to see flex had cooked her breakfast.

"Oh, wow what's this all about buddy." Sharday says as she sits down at the table.

"You was tired, and I figured when you woke up you would be hungry, That's all." Flex says as he smiles.

"Mmmm...hmm....thanks I appreciate it though." Sharday says as she walks in the washroom to wash her face and put toothpaste on her finger and finger brushed her teeth. Smiled and walked back into kitchen to hear her phone ringing as soon as she sit down.

"Your phone ringing." Flex tells her.

"I'll get it in a min." Sharday says as she smiles.

So, while Sharday and Flex was eating Flex stopped chewing.

"You know its ok to answer your phone and reply to messages while we are together it's not a problem." Flex says as Sharday looked at him and stop chewing.

"I know but I try to respectful to your time and not be in my phone while I'm with you, that's all." Sharday says.

Flex laughs

"I appreciate that but actually its really, really cool because I'm the type of nigga that will just start eating your pussy while you're on the phone and I bet you won't be on it long after." Flex says as Sharday laughs and giggles as she stirs her rice and smiles.

"Oh really, so your saying if I'm on the phone with my mom you're going to start eating my pussy.

"Yea should I show some kind of respect because it's your mom."

"I would think." Sharday says as she leans her neck back in shock.

"Fukk that mom on my time and I do what I gotta do to get your undivided attention by any means." Flex says aggressively.

"Well damn my nigga I don't know how I should take that." Sharday says in shock.

"Exactly how I gave it to you, in the rawest form, that's how gotdammit."

"Wow." Sharday says in more shock, but she kind of likes his aggression.

So after they finish eating they sat there and talked for a little while before Sharday left and headed home, but on her way out she gave flex a hug and he cuffed her ass and spreaded her cheeks and to his surprise her pussy lips made that lip smacking noise when he did that and she smiled as he grinned as he watched he walk away and get in her car and pull off.

"Aw I will be back, so when we can have that talk to."

"Yea, Yea whatever." Flex says as he throws his hand at her.

"You think I'm playing I see." Sharday says as she laughs and gets in her car.

On the other side of town, Zella wipes sweat and says wait make it cry wtf that mean Zack smiles.

So, after holding up Zella while fukking her and Making her cum multiple times he throws her on the bed and say let me show you what I mean, then he stands up in her pussy and his dick is harder than Chinese arithmetic, she laughs, smiles and he grabs her ankles pulls her to the edge of the bed, the takes both of her legs and pushes her knees to her shoulders.

"Hold them ankles baby." Zack says as she does just that as he slaps his dick on her pussy three times, inserts it slowly then slow strokes her to death until his dick had a paint job. She came three times more and squirted (I mean cried) before zack even had a chance to cum, but after 20 minutes he finally did they both rolled over and went to sleep.

Zack and Zella was sleeping so well, neither one of them heard their phones ringing.

Zella had two missed calls and three messages. While Zack had one missed call and two messages. Sharday was the two missed calls and two of the messages.

Sharday first message read.

"I need to talk to you about yo boy Flex."

And the second one read.

"I'll just head over to mom house in the a.m. and wait on you cause eventually you will stop by there." Sharday says. But what she don't know is that's where her and Zack are laid up at.

Ok since Zella mom knows Sharday, she will let her in the house with no problem.

So as Sharday pulls up to Zella house.

"Wait that looks like Zack's car," Sharday says come to Find out it is his car she calls Zella again, no answer, she hangs up.

As soon as she tries to call Zack its interrupted because Zella calls her back.

"What's up girl." Zella says.

"Shit sleepy head wyd, you woke now."

"Just Woke up, what's going on."

"I'm in the front open the door."

"Aight, here I come."

Zella opens door for Sharday but as soon as Sharday came in Zella saw the look on her face, like she was looking for something or someone.

"You got company.' Sharday asks as she walked in.

Zella smiles, grins, and giggles

"Yes, and what's wrong with you Sharday, you good."

Sharday looks at her smiles and ask her.

"Is Zack here."

Zella smiles and giggles.

"Yes."

Sharday smiles, giggles, and laughs.

"Mmmm, hmm what you up." Sharday asks her while smiling.

"Up to, nothing." Zella says as she smiles while giggling.

"Wait a minute I know that giggle."

"What giggle." Zella says as she laughs.

Sharday points at the smirk on her Zella face, right after Zella smiles.

"Wait a minute." Sharday says as she pushes Zella on the couch and sits down next to her.

Zella looks shocked as she smiles and laughs.

"Wait a minute, was Zack here last night." Sharday asks.

"Was, he still here." Zella says as she smiles.

"Wait he spent the night." Sharday asks while smiling.

Zella smiles looks at Sharday laughs and smirks, then laughs.

"Yea." Zella says as she smiles.

Sharday laughs and hits her on the shoulder.

"You gave him the pussy didn't you." Sharday asks he with the shocked face as she puts her hands on her waist.

"Yes and no." Zella says as she smiles.

Sharday looks shocked and surprised.

"You gave it to him, and he took it huh."

Zella smiles, laughs, and giggles.

"Hell yea." Zella says and right after, Sharday gets a call from Diego and text from O Damn. She ignored the call and didn't reply to the message.

"So how was it, did you like it, was you satisfied or disappointed, spill the beans hoe." Sharday says as she folds her arms and smiles.

"Girl, girl, girl let me tell you." Zella says but she didn't get a chance to go into the details because Zack walked in the room, so she changed the subject.

"Yea girl so they want me to work this weekend, but I said I can't because I have a prior engagement that I have to attend to, because it's already paid for.

"And why do they always wait till the day before you are off to ask yall to come in to work, I hate that shit, omg." Sharday says as she grins.

"Sharday what's happening." Zack says as he smiles at Sharday as she smiles and giggles.

"What's up Zack long time no see, how you been."

"I been cooling how you been."

"I been good I can't complain."

"That's good to hear, well Zella I'm going to head out now, was good seeing you Sharday.

"Same here Zack." Sharday says as she smiles.

"Zella imma head to the house I'll see ya later Zack. Sharday says as she smiles.

"Nice seeing you Sharday." Zack says as he smiles

Sharday moves her lips and tells Zella she will call her as she heads out the house after Zack leaves and calls Diego back as she sees that Flex and O'Dell texted her.

"Wyd." Sharday says.

"Chilling, waiting on you." Flex says.

"Oh Really." Sharday says as she sends smiling emoji.

"Hell yea, so hurry up and bring me that pussy." Flex says.

"Omw." Sharday says as she sits in car and looks at Zack as he pulls off as he winks his eye at her before he pulled off, and smiles as she gets a text from O'Dell

"Lets the games begin." O'Dell says after sending laughing emojis.

"Bet' em up, let's get it." Sharday says as she smiles.

To be continued.......

Coming soon

Romantic War 2: Love is War

Poetic Journey

Single Until you're Married

Bullets Talk

Sex Assassin 2: Pleasured Punishment